The Crow and the Peacock

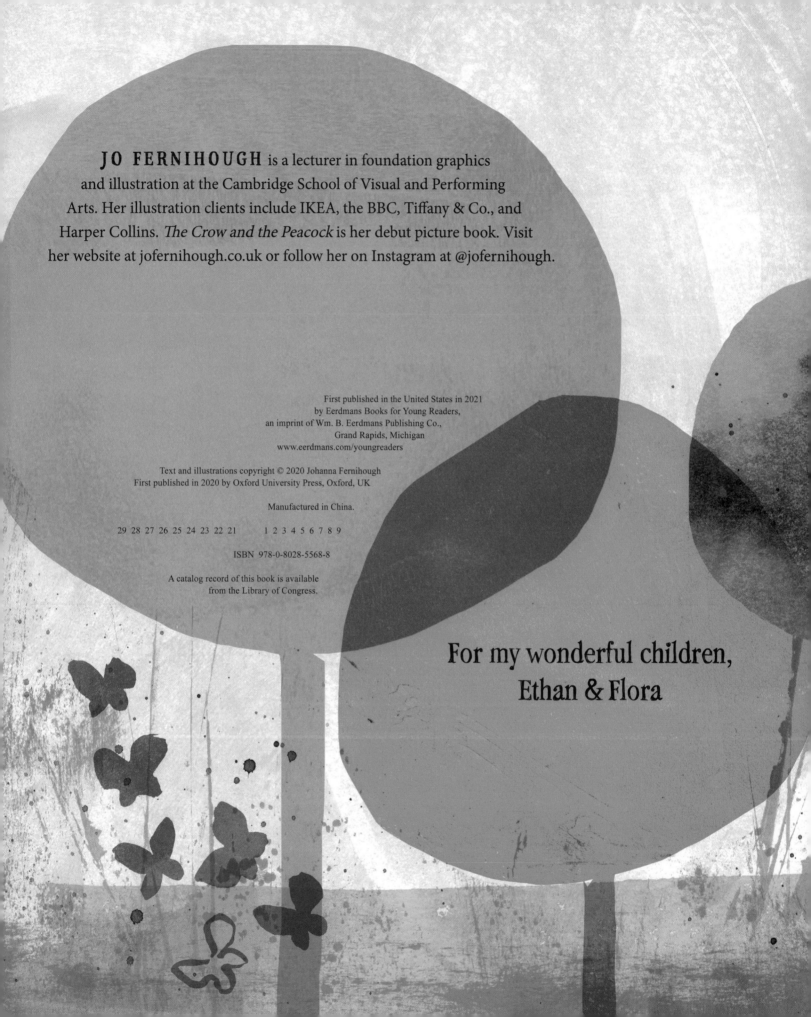

JO FERNIHOUGH is a lecturer in foundation graphics and illustration at the Cambridge School of Visual and Performing Arts. Her illustration clients include IKEA, the BBC, Tiffany & Co., and Harper Collins. *The Crow and the Peacock* is her debut picture book. Visit her website at jofernihough.co.uk or follow her on Instagram at @jofernihough.

First published in the United States in 2021
by Eerdmans Books for Young Readers,
an imprint of Wm. B. Eerdmans Publishing Co.,
Grand Rapids, Michigan
www.eerdmans.com/youngreaders

Text and illustrations copyright © 2020 Johanna Fernihough
First published in 2020 by Oxford University Press, Oxford, UK

Manufactured in China.

29 28 27 26 25 24 23 22 21   1 2 3 4 5 6 7 8 9

ISBN 978-0-8028-5568-8

A catalog record of this book is available
from the Library of Congress.

For my wonderful children,
Ethan & Flora

The Crow and the Peacock

JO FERNIHOUGH

EERDMANS BOOKS FOR YOUNG READERS

GRAND RAPIDS, MICHIGAN

There was once a crow
who lived in the woods.

Crow was happy with his
life and never wanted
for anything, until . . .

. . . one day,
Crow saw a dove.
She was cooing
softly from her nest.

That bird is so beautiful and her cooing is so soothing, thought Crow.

Her bright feathers make mine seem so dull, and who would want to listen to my loud "caw caw"?

Crow flew up to the
dove and said,
"You're so beautiful.
You must be the
happiest bird alive."

"I thought I was happy," said Dove, "until I heard Nightingale sing. His singing is so magnificent, it makes my cooing sound plain.

"Nightingale must be the happiest bird in the world."

"Your singing is so magnificent," said Crow. "You must be the happiest bird alive."

"I thought I was happy," said Nightingale, "until I met Rooster . . .

"Every morning, his call is heard across the land. Yet my song is heard by only a few in the night. Rooster must be the happiest bird in the world."

The next morning,
Crow flew to the farm
to meet Rooster.

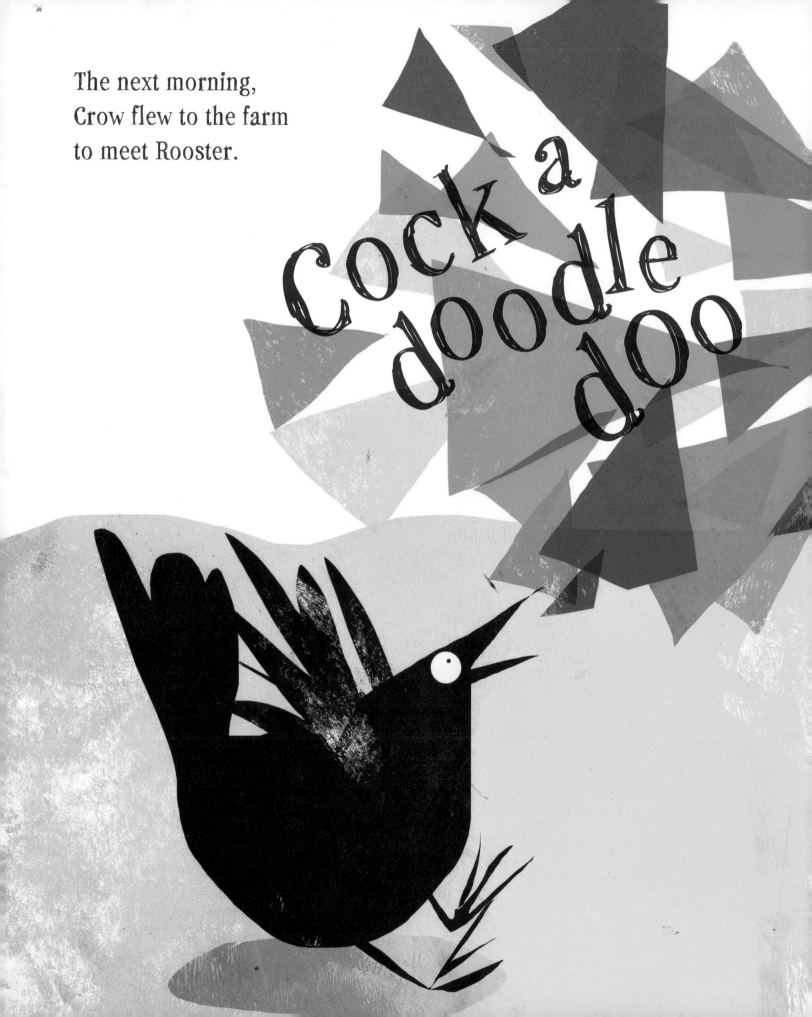

"Your call is so famous," said Crow. "You must be the happiest bird alive."

"I thought I was happy," said Rooster, "until I met Swan . . .

"Swan spends all day swimming on the cool river, while I must live on this dusty and hot farm. Swan must be the happiest bird in the world."

Crow flew to the river to see Swan.

"Your river is a beautiful place to live," said Crow. "You must be the happiest bird alive."

"I thought I was happy," said
Swan, "but then I met Peacock . . .

". . . Peacock wears the crown of
a majestic king, and his feathers
sparkle like jewels.
Next to him, I'm so ordinary.

"Peacock must be the happiest bird in the world."

Crow couldn't wait
to meet Peacock.

At first he had
trouble seeing over
the huge crowd
that had gathered
around.

But when the
crowd finally left,
Crow hopped over
to take a closer
look . . .

Ooohhh beautiful

"Oh, WOW!

You truly are the king
of birds! You MUST be the
happiest bird alive."

Peacock sighed and said, "I was once happy. I used to call to the monsoons from high on my tree . . .

" . . . but then the emperor put me in a cage
so his people could admire my beauty."

Peacock looked at the sky.
"Every day I see crows
flying free—and all I
want to be is a crow.

"I think you, Crow, must be
the happiest bird alive."

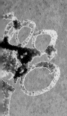

Crow flew back to the woods feeling content with his dark feathers and shrill call.

He knew for certain that he
was happy with his life and
now all he wanted . . .

. . . was to share his happiness
in whatever way he could.